Adventures with Barbie™ 

Ballet Debut

Suzanne Weyn

PRICE STERN SLOAN
Los Angeles

For my little love
Diana Weyn Gonzalez

Published by Price Stern Sloan, Inc.
11150 Olympic Boulevard
Los Angeles, California 90064
ISBN: 0-8431-3410-0
Printed in the United States of America
10 9 8 7 6 5 4 3 2

Contents

1

Ballet Class

Barbie stood on the corner of a busy city block. All around her, people hurried and traffic rumbled by. There it is, she thought excitedly. Across the street was a sign over a doorway. It read: Worldwide Ballet School.

As she crossed, Barbie's heart pounded. She'd been accepted as a student at the most famous ballet school in the country.

Inside the door was a small lobby. A secretary sat at a long wooden desk. "Hi, I'm Barbie, and this is my first class."

The secretary opened a large notebook. "Here you are," she said, pointing to Barbie's name on a long list. "You will be studying with Lisa Saint John."

"The famous Lisa Saint John?" Barbie gasped.

The woman smiled. "Madame Saint John doesn't dance anymore. But she is one of our best teachers."

Now Barbie was more excited than ever. "Where can I change?" she asked.

"The ladies' dressing room is at the end of that hallway," the secretary said, pointing. "Madame Saint John's class is to your right."

"Thank you," said Barbie. Clutching her pink dance bag, she hurried down the hall.

In the dressing room, she quickly changed into her new sparkly pink leotard and tights. She pulled on her soft pink ballet practice shoes and tied back her long golden hair.

A mirror hung on the wall. She gazed into it. Her own big blue eyes looked back at her. "OK, Barbie," she said to her image. "You did it! You made it into the best school in the country!"

Barbie had studied at a local ballet school since she was little. But this was different.

Now she would be studying with the finest dancers anywhere.

When she got to the studio, fifteen other students were busy warming up. They stood at a long wooden pole that ran along one wall. The pole was called a *barre* (BAR). The wall across from it was one big mirror. The dancers used the mirror to make sure they were doing their movements properly.

In advanced ballet lessons, the dancers join the class at different times. Some of the students in this class had been enrolled for many weeks. Barbie would have to try to keep up with them.

She found a spot at the barre and held on with one hand. She began warming up with simple ballet movements.

Soon Madame Saint John entered the room. She was a small woman, and very old. Her white hair was pulled back in a bun, and she wore a plain black dress.

"We will have a special guest with us for the next few weeks," the teacher told the class. "Ivan Stavinsky."

A murmur of excitement spread through the room. Ivan Stavinsky was the most famous ballet star in America. Six years before, he had sneaked away from his Russian dance company—the Bolshoi Ballet. The company had been touring in the United States. After one week, the dancers were supposed to return to Russia. But Ivan wanted to stay. That was a problem. Back then, Russians couldn't leave Russia.

The day the dancers were supposed to fly home, Ivan disappeared. The company left without him. He went on to become a star of American ballet.

"Ivan is in town working on his role as the Prince in *The Nutcracker Suite*." Madame Saint John said. "When he is not busy with the show, he will study with us."

Just then, the famous dancer entered. He was handsome, with blond hair and dark eyes. He wore a black one-piece leotard.

The dancer bowed his head politely to the class. As he walked farther into the room, he noticed Barbie. The moment he saw her, he froze. Then he went pale. Confused by his actions, Barbie smiled. Ivan just looked past her and walked on. How strange, thought Barbie.

Madame Saint John began class. Barbie had no trouble keeping up with the other students.

But throughout the class, Barbie saw Ivan Stavinsky glancing at her. The moment she caught him looking at her, he would look away.

Madame Saint John told the students that today they would work on a *pas de deux* (PA-DE-DU). The French term meant a romantic dance between a man and a woman.

The class paired off quickly. Since they were both new, only Barbie and Ivan were left. Madame Saint John led Barbie over to Ivan. "You two will be partners," she told Ivan.

Ivan frowned. "No!" he snapped. "I refuse to dance with this woman. Not now. Not ever!"

2

A Mysterious Letter

"It was awful!" Barbie told her boyfriend, Ken, and her sister, Skipper.

"Did Ivan Stavinsky say why he wouldn't dance with you?" asked Ken.

"He said that I was clumsy!"

"That's not very nice," Skipper grumbled.

"I guess that was why he kept looking at me—because I was so bad. And I thought I was doing pretty well, too!"

"I don't think that was why," Ken said. "You told us he looked at you strangely even before you began dancing."

"That's true," said Barbie.

"Don't let him get to you," Skipper said. "Who does he think he is, anyway?"

"Only the greatest dancer in the country, possibly the world," Barbie answered.

"I guess that's true," Skipper said. She got up and hugged Barbie. "But you're Barbie, the greatest big sister in the world.

"Thanks, Skipper," said Barbie.

Ken glanced at the clock. "I'd better be getting home," he said. Barbie walked Ken to the front door. "I almost dread going back to class," she confessed.

Ken put his arm around her. "You've worked hard for this, Barbie. And you're good. Don't let him get you down."

After Ken said good night, Barbie went upstairs to her bedroom. Ken is right, she thought as she got into bed. She wasn't going to let Ivan Stavinsky upset her.

Barbie awoke eager to go to her next class. Still, when she got to the Worldwide Ballet School, she was glad to see that Ivan Stavinsky was not there.

Madame Saint John stopped Barbie at the door as she entered class. "I hope you are not upset about yesterday. Ivan will be busy with the show for a while," said the kind teacher. "You won't have to think about him for the next couple of days."

That day Barbie had a great class. She left feeling good about herself. "Excuse me," the secretary called as Barbie passed her desk. "You wouldn't be going by the City Center Theater, would you?"

"I am, yes," Barbie told her.

"Would you take this letter to Ivan?" The secretary held out a white envelope. "It was sent here to the school, but Ivan won't be in for a couple of days. I want to make sure he gets it."

Ivan! Oh, no, thought Barbie. She looked at the address. "But this is supposed to go to someone in Russia."

"Ivan mailed it to Russia, but the post office returned it," the woman explained. Sure enough, the return name was Ivan Stavinsky.

"I'll deliver it," Barbie said. She wasn't going to spend her life being afraid of Ivan.

Outside, the wind whipped dry leaves around the street. Barbie kept one hand on her hat as she walked to the City Center Theater.

When she reached the building, she walked up the steps. In the lobby, she heard the lovely music of *The Nutcracker Suite*.

Barbie stepped into the auditorium. At center stage with Ivan was Ilsa Strauss. Barbie had seen her perform once.

For a while, Barbie sat in the last row and watched Ivan and Ilsa rehearse. Although the stage was bare, she was swept up in the music and the grace of the dancers.

Just then, Ivan stumbled slightly. The director, a tall, thin man, jumped out of his front-row seat. "Stop!" he yelled.

The music ceased and the dancers stood still. "Ivan!" the director cried. "You are all off today. You're not with us."

Ivan shrugged miserably. "Let's try it again," he said. "Give me a moment."

"Ten-minute break!" the director's aide cried. The dancers began leaving the stage. This would be a good time to give Ivan his letter.

Barbie hurried down the aisle. Ivan was slumped in a seat near the front. He seemed deep in thought. "Hello," she said.

"You again!" he cried, startled.

"The secretary at the school asked me to give you this," she said, handing him the envelope.

When Ivan saw the letter, the color drained from his face. His eyes were filled with anger. "It would be you who brings me this letter!" he cried, leaping to his feet.

"I'm just delivering it," Barbie said.

"Get away from me!" Ivan barked at her. With that, he turned and stormed off.

3

Barbie Finds a Clue

The next day Ivan wasn't in class again. Barbie had a wonderful, exciting time.

But on the third day, he was there. With her head high, she walked by without giving him a glance.

Yet she could feel him constantly staring at her. It made her turn. When she did, she would see his eyes fixed on her.

What's going on? Barbie wondered. He doesn't like me, yet he can't stop looking at me. This is very strange. Barbie decided she was going to find out what was happening. And she was going to find out today.

After class Ivan hurried out of the room. "Darn!" said Barbie, running into the hall. He was nowhere in sight. He must be changing, she figured. I can catch him on the way out.

Barbie went into the women's dressing room. "What's with you and Ivan?" asked one of the dancers. "He keeps staring at you. Are you guys friends or enemies?"

"I wish I could answer your question," Barbie replied. "But I barely know Ivan."

The dancer shrugged. "You know how artists are—very odd sometimes."

"I guess," said Barbie. But something told her there was more to it. Ivan didn't seem odd with anyone else. Barbie changed quickly into her regular clothes—a pair of flowered leggings, a red mini and a yellow sweater—and left the dressing room in time to see Ivan coming out of the men's dressing room.

"Ivan," she called, but he didn't appear to hear her. Instead, he walked quickly down the hall toward the door.

Catching up to him, Barbie reached out and put her hand on his shoulder. Ivan whirled around, dropping the folder he held under his arm. "Now see what you've done," he growled. He knelt to gather the fallen papers.

"I'm very sorry," said Barbie. "But I only wanted to talk to you."

He looked up at her. For a split second his face softened. Then it hardened once again. "What could you possibly have to talk to me about?" he asked, getting to his feet.

"I want to know why you've been so nasty to me," Barbie said. "I've never done anything to you."

Ivan's eyes were cold. "That's what you think. But you have no idea."

"Please explain what you mean," Barbie pressed.

"You wouldn't understand," he grumbled. Abruptly, he turned and walked away.

That didn't tell me much, she thought. At that moment, something on the floor caught her eye. It was a white square of paper, the back of a photo. Barbie stooped to pick it up.

Perhaps it had fallen from Ivan's folder.

"Oh, my gosh!" Barbie gasped when she turned the photo over. She couldn't believe her eyes! The photo was of a young woman. And she looked exactly like Barbie!

The woman stood in a snow-covered park wrapped in a heavy coat and hat. Her large, blue eyes gazed up brightly. Blond bangs peeked out from under her hat. A long blond braid trailed down the front of her coat.

"It's me, but, of course, it's not me," Barbie whispered.

Breaking into a run, Barbie went after Ivan. She clattered down the steps and met up with him at the curb. He was trying to hail a cab, but no one was stopping.

"I see that even the great Ivan Stavinsky can't always get a cab," she teased, coming up alongside him.

"What is it now?" he grumbled.

She held the photo out to him. "I think you dropped this."

"So now you know why I dislike you so much," Ivan said with a joyless laugh.

"Not exactly," Barbie admitted. "Did this person hurt you very badly?"

"She didn't mean to," Ivan said with a sad smile. "But when I think of her, the pain is very great. That is why I cannot bear to see you. It reminds me of her."

"Would you like to talk about it?" Barbie asked, sensing that he needed someone to talk to.

"I never speak of this," he said.

"All right," said Barbie, turning away.

She headed down the block. At least now she had some idea why Ivan acted as he did. Whatever was troubling him must be very painful.

Suddenly Barbie heard Ivan calling out to her. "Wait!" he shouted, running to catch up. "Maybe I would like to talk, after all."

4

The Truth Unfolds

Barbie wrapped her hands around her mug of hot cocoa. She and Ivan sat talking in a nearby coffee shop. He had begun his story by telling her about his early training with the Bolshoi Ballet.

"They were grooming Valeria and me to be top dancers," he said. "It was an honor."

"Valeria?" Barbie asked.

"Yes," said Ivan. "She is the woman in the picture. She was my dance partner. And she is my sister."

"Your sister!" Barbie gasped. "I thought perhaps she was your girlfriend."

Ivan shook his head. "I begged her to stay in the United States with me. But she was scared. It broke my heart to leave her. I had to go, though. I needed my freedom as an artist.

I could find it only in America."

"It must have been a hard choice," Barbie said kindly.

"The hardest in my life," Ivan said. "At the time, I feared that the government would think Valeria had helped me escape. I knew they would be watching her, so I did not write to her for five years. I didn't write to my parents, either. I wanted to make sure nothing bad happened to them because of my actions."

"And you couldn't go back to see them," said Barbie. "Not ever."

"No. I would have been jailed as a traitor to my country."

"But now things have changed in Russia," said Barbie. "The Communists are gone. The borders are opening more and more every day. Why don't you go back now?"

"I would, in a second," said Ivan. "But through the years my family has moved about. I don't know where to find them. The letter you returned to me was my tenth attempt to contact them. I thought I had found them, but the envelope said, 'No longer at this address.' "

"No wonder you were so upset," said Barbie. "I had no idea."

"You couldn't have known," said Ivan. "It was written in Russian."

"Could you find your sister through your contacts in the ballet world?"

"I wrote the head of the Bolshoi. For some reason, Valeria is no longer dancing there. He is a new director and knew no more than that. This worries me. Why is she no longer there? Is she ill, hurt...dead?"

Barbie reached across the table and touched Ivan's arm. "I don't know what I would do if I couldn't find my sister, Skipper," she said. "I can imagine how you feel."

"It's like a pain that bothers me every day," he said, his voice full of emotion. In a moment, he forced a small smile. "I am sorry to burden you with my problems. And after I have been such a bear to you, too."

"It's all right," Barbie said. "I can't help looking like your sister, though."

"No. I have a thought," said Ivan. "Instead of being sad, I will be happy. For a short time I will be able to pretend that I have my sister with me again. I will look at it as a pleasure, not a pain."

"But you must remember that I am not Valeria," Barbie warned.

"Don't worry. I will remember that," Ivan said. "Thank you for listening. Oh, and one more thing. You are not in the least clumsy. I simply did not know what else to say."

Barbie smiled. "Thanks for telling me that."

"Now I really must get to the theater. I think I will dance better than I have in days."

"Is it because of me that you haven't been doing well?" Barbie asked.

"I'm afraid so," Ivan replied. "Seeing you has stirred up old feelings of homesickness. My mind was not on my work. But now that we have talked, I feel better."

"I'm glad," said Barbie.

As they stepped out of the coffee shop, a bitter wind swirled around them. Barbie shivered. "Brrr—winter weather will be here very soon, it seems."

"Of course," Ivan grinned. "When we start dancing *The Nutcracker*, you know the holidays are coming. I love winter. It reminds me of home."

Just then, someone called out to Ivan from across the street. Barbie saw Ilsa Strauss waving. "Ivan, wait," Ilsa called. "I'll walk to the theater with you."

With a bright smile, the young woman dashed into the street. At the same time, Barbie saw a truck turn the corner.

"Ilsa! Look out!" Barbie screamed.

The ballerina's happy eyes filled with panic. For a split second, she froze. Then she leapt backward, throwing herself onto the sidewalk.

Barbie and Ivan raced to her.

"Are you all right?" asked Ivan, kneeling beside the fallen ballerina.

Ilsa frowned in pain. "It's my ankle! I think my ankle is broken!"

5

Barbie's Tough Choice

City Hospital was filled with people. "They sure are busy," noted Barbie. She sat beside Ivan on a brown couch in the waiting area. "It was lucky they took Ilsa so quickly."

"It is luckier still that you saw the truck coming," said Ivan.

As they spoke, Ilsa entered the room leaning on a cane. Her ankle was wrapped in a large bandage. "It's not broken," she told Barbie and Ivan. "But it's a bad sprain. They told me to stay off it for two weeks."

"Two weeks!" cried Ivan.

"I know," moaned Ilsa. "The ballet opens in a week and a half. I won't be able to dance. I'll be letting everyone down." She began to cry.

"Don't cry," said Barbie, handing her a tissue. "These things happen."

Ilsa wiped her tears. "All the leading dancers are busy," she said through her sniffs. "You'll never find someone else at this date."

Outside the hospital, they hailed a cab and dropped Ilsa off at her apartment.

"What will happen to the show now?" Barbie asked Ivan as the driver took them toward her house.

"The show won't open if we can't replace Ilsa," he said, frowning.

"There must be lots of aspiring ballerinas who'd love to dance the role," said Barbie.

"How about you?" Ivan asked.

"Me?" Barbie gasped.

"Yes, you," he said. "You're a natural talent. You have the grace and the strength. We will have to go with a new ballerina, no matter what. You are my choice. The director will listen to me."

Barbie was shocked. "I...I couldn't," she said. "I'm not ready...I don't know the role."

"I will teach you what you need to know," Ivan insisted.

"Here you are," said the driver, pulling up in front of Barbie's house.

"Can I give you my answer in the morning?" Barbie asked Ivan.

"Of course. Here, take my card," he said, handing her a business card. "It has my home number on it. Call me the moment you make up your mind."

Barbie took the card and got out of the cab. She climbed her steps and unlocked the front door. Ken and Skipper were sitting on the living room floor in front of the TV. They were playing a video game. "Hi," Barbie said, stepping into the room.

"Hi," Ken replied, looking away from the screen. "I came by to see if you wanted to go out tonight. I figured you'd be home by now. Is everything OK?"

Skipper turned to Barbie. "Hey, are you all

right, Barbie? You look a little worried."

"I'm fine," Barbie assured them. "I have some big news, though." She sat on her couch and told them all that had happened.

"You're going to be a star!" Skipper shouted excitedly. "Way to go, Barbie!"

"Wait a minute," said Barbie. "I don't know yet. I'm not sure I'm good enough."

"Ivan wouldn't have asked if he didn't think you'd be good," Ken said.

"I don't know," said Barbie doubtfully.

"Barbie," said Skipper sternly. "Do you remember when I had the lead in the school play?"

"Of course," said Barbie.

"Don't you remember how nervous I was? You told me to hang in there. You said that I was good enough if I believed I was."

"And I was right," Barbie recalled. "You were wonderful."

"Well, now I'm telling you the same thing.

You're as good as you want to be. This is a great chance, Barbie. Do you want to live your whole life thinking that you could have danced with Ivan Stavinsky—but you were too chicken?"

"I am not chicken!" Barbie said.

Skipper tucked her hands under her armpits and flapped her arms as if they were wings. "Buck, buck, baaa!" she clucked.

"Stop that," Barbie said, laughing.

"Chicken! Chicken! Chicken!" Skipper teased, dancing around and flapping her arms.

"That does it," said Barbie, smiling. She got up and took Ivan's card from the pocket of her jacket. Then she went to the phone and punched in the number.

Ivan wasn't home yet, but his phone machine answered. "Hello, Ivan," Barbie said after the tone. "This is Barbie. I've made my decision. I'd love to take the role of Clara in *The Nutcracker*."

6

Startling News

"You must trust me to catch you, Barbie," Ivan coached. "Try it again."

It was Barbie's first day at the City Center. She was already learning steps that were more difficult than any she had tried before.

She'd spent the last hour working on a leap into Ivan's arms. She tried, but she couldn't trust Ivan to catch her.

You've got to do it this time, she told herself. If you fall on your face, then you fall on your face. You'll live.

Barbie began the series of light steps. Then, calling up all her courage, she leapt.

"Got you!" Ivan whispered as she landed in his outstretched arms. In the next moment, he lifted her over his head.

The cast and crew clapped. "Lovely! Perfect!"

shouted the director, Tony Ramirez. "That's enough for today."

"I knew you'd get it," Ivan said.

"I wasn't so sure," Barbie replied.

Looking out into the theater, Barbie spotted Ken waiting for her. "I need a minute to change," she called to him.

She ran to the dressing room and washed up. Then she put on a furry blue sweater and a silky white skirt. She and Ken were going to a play that night.

Soon she was ready. She hurried back to where Ken was waiting. His jeep was parked outside. They climbed in and drove downtown.

"My muscles ache," Barbie confessed.

"You were doing great, though," Ken said proudly. "That last leap was awesome."

"Thank goodness I finally got it right," said Barbie. "I thought I'd never be able to do it."

"I know you, Barbie," Ken said, chuckling. "You never give up."

The play was a comedy. Barbie laughed until her sides hurt.

"I'm starved. Let's get something to eat," said Ken when the play was over.

"Ivan told me about a really good Russian restaurant around here," Barbie said. "It's called Uri's."

"Let's try it," said Ken. "I've never had Russian food."

"Neither have I," said Barbie, pulling on her pink coat.

Uri's was busy and loud. Waiters rushed about while customers laughed and sang.

"Purple soup?" Ken questioned nervously when their first course arrived.

"Well, we ordered beet soup. I suppose it should be reddish purple," said Barbie. She sipped some. "It's wonderful!"

They enjoyed all of their meal and were about to order dessert when an old woman approached their table. She was tall and thin.

Her silver hair was piled in a topknot.

"Valeria," she said with a heavy Russian accent. She took Barbie's hand and pressed it warmly. "I did not know you were coming to America. When did you arrive?"

"I'm sorry, but you're mistaken," Barbie told her politely. "I'm Barbie."

"Oh, my heavens," the woman gasped, letting go of Barbie's hand. "I beg your pardon. But you look exactly like—"

"I know," Barbie cut in, smiling. "I look like Valeria Stavinsky. Her brother told me."

"You know Ivan, then," said the woman. "It is such a shame the way he has cut himself off from his family."

"He felt he had to," Barbie told her. "Is Valeria all right? Ivan is worried."

"She's fine," the woman replied. "Now she dances with a smaller company. It is less demanding."

"Do you know where she is?" Barbie asked.

"Of course. I know her well. At home, her parents were my neighbors."

"Would you write down her address for me?" Barbie asked. The woman wrote it on a napkin. "Thank you," Barbie said.

"You are welcome," the woman replied. "Tell that boy to write his mama. She thinks he no longer cares about them."

"That's not true," Barbie told her. "He cares very much.

"I wish I could see his face when you give him that address," said Ken after the woman had left.

Barbie folded the napkin and put it into her purse. "I may not give it to him just yet," she said, a mysterious look in her blue eyes.

"What?" cried Ken.

"He's waited this long for the address. He can wait a little longer," she said.

"Barbie, what's going on?" Ken asked.

Barbie smiled at him. "You'll see."

7

Thoughts of Home

The next week was a very busy one. Day after day Barbie worked hard to perfect her ballet steps. There were also long, boring practices when the crew checked the lights and the sound. In addition, Barbie had several fittings with the costume designer, Mrs. Hill.

"Clara dances most of the ballet in her nightgown," explained Mrs. Hill. "So we must make sure it is the most gorgeous nightgown ever."

Barbie stood patiently while Mrs. Hill fitted the nightgown to her. It had a blue top made of sparkly fabric covered with stars. The gauzy blue skirt flowed in layers down to her calves.

"It's so lovely," Barbie sighed.

"We'll put this in your hair," said Mrs. Hill. She cut a yard of sparkly blue ribbon from a

spool. Skillfully, she tied it around Barbie's beautiful long hair.

Then Mrs. Hill reached into her big black canvas bag. "Now for the best part," she said. Out came a pair of blue toe shoes.

Barbie tried them on. She crisscrossed the soft ribbons around her ankles, then tied the ends in a bow.

"Work in those shoes from now on," Mrs. Hill told her. "They need to be broken in."

"I'll never take them off," Barbie said, laughing.

"You look like a dream," said Mrs. Hill. "Now you'd better get out there."

Barbie hurried from the dressing room to the stage. The final pieces of the stage set had been put into place. All around her, the dancers walked by in their costumes. Some were dressed as giant mice, others were sugar plum fairies, snowflakes, jesters—it was magical and thrilling beyond words.

Ivan walked toward her from across the stage. He was dressed as the Prince in blue tights and a short blue jacket with stars, just like the stars on Barbie's costume. "You look great," Barbie told him, smiling.

But Ivan did not return her smile. "It is amazing," he said, walking around her. "You look exactly like Valeria when she played Clara. Exactly!"

"I wish I could meet her," said Barbie.

Ivan nodded sadly. "I wish you could, too. You would be great friends."

For a moment, Barbie felt guilty about not giving Ivan the address. Should she tell him? No. She would stick with her plan.

Just then, a crew member walked up to them. "I want to see how the lighting looks with the snow," he told them. "Could you stand by the open window?"

"Sure," said Barbie.

She and Ivan walked to a huge window frame in the middle of the set. In the ballet, Clara shrinks to the size of the tiny Nutcracker Prince. So the window had to seem very big.

When Barbie and Ivan were in place, the stage lights dimmed. A blue spotlight was directed at them. "Turn on the snow!" the crew member shouted.

From a platform above the stage, a fan was quietly turned on. It sent a shower of feathery white soap flakes raining down. Barbie recalled what Ivan had told her. Snow reminded him of home. The pain in his face told her he was thinking of home now.

"Are you all right?" she asked him.

Ivan smiled at her warmly. "Don't tell anyone," he said.

"Tell what?"

"That the great Ivan Stavinsky is just a homesick boy, after all."

Barbie squeezed his arm. "Your secret is safe with me," she said, gently.

"The snow looks super!" the crew member shouted. The bright stage lights were snapped on, and the mood was broken.

"Now we want to test the spotlights," yelled the lighting director.

As Barbie brushed the soap flakes from the window ledge, she sighed. "When do we get back to dancing?"

"Soon," Ivan said, laughing. "The next few days are going to seem very, very long. There's still so much to do."

Barbie discovered that Ivan was telling the truth. It was an exhausting day. By seven that evening she was very tired. "That's it for today," announced Tony Ramirez. Thank goodness, thought Barbie as she hurried to the pay phone in the lobby.

Quickly, she dialed her home number. "Hi, Skipper, it's me," she said when her sister picked up the phone. "Was there anything from Russia in the mail?"

"Yes, it arrived!" cried Skipper.

8

The Plan Goes Wrong

Barbie steered her pink 1957 Chevy through the late-afternoon traffic. She checked her watch and smiled. She still had plenty of time to get to the airport and back.

Running late would mean a disaster. Tonight was opening night! Barbie had to be at the theater by six-thirty. She needed to be dressed, in her makeup and warmed up by eight. That was when the curtain went up.

But right now she had a plane to meet. On it were some very important people—Valeria and Ivan's parents.

Barbie's letter from Russia had been from Ivan's sister. Barbie had written her a letter, and she had written back. Valeria's letter was written in slightly stiff English. She said she was thrilled to learn that Ivan wanted to see her. All this time she had thought that he was angry with her for not staying behind with him.

After that, Barbie and Valeria exchanged letters by overnight mail. There was no time to lose. On her end, Barbie made travel plans. She used her earnings from the ballet to help pay for the plane tickets. For her part, Valeria got the needed papers and passports. Barbie wished she could have gotten the Stavinskys an earlier flight. But this was the best the airlines could do.

Barbie parked in the airport lot and hurried to the main terminal. The flight from Russia would arrive an hour late.

Stay calm, she told herself. You still have lots of time.

In an hour, the jumbo jet set down. Barbie waited at the gate. Finally, Valeria Stavinsky came through the door. Barbie gasped. It was like looking in the mirror!

As in the photo, the young woman wore her

blond hair in a long braid. She carried a heavy coat over her arm. "Barbie!" she cried.

Without a thought, she and Barbie hugged. "I always wondered what it would be like to have a twin sister," said Barbie. "Now I know!"

"Yes! Yes!" said Valeria, laughing excitedly. "I, too, wondered."

Behind Valeria was a short, broad-shouldered man. He had the same large, dark eyes as Ivan. At his side was a tall, thin woman with an aged but beautiful face. "Welcome to America," Barbie said warmly. For a moment the Stavinskys simply stared, wide-eyed. Barbie looked so much like Valeria. Then they broke into happy smiles and spoke joyfully in Russian."They thank you from the bottom of their hearts," Valeria explained.

"Tell them they are very welcome," Barbie said. "Doing this gives me great pleasure."

Once again, Barbie checked her watch. "We'll stop at my house first. You can rest and wash up. My boyfriend, Ken, will bring you to the theater."

The Stavinskys followed Barbie to the baggage-claim area. Barbie tried not to worry, but the arrival of their luggage was taking a long time. "Do you still wish to go through with plan B?" Valeria asked as they waited.

"Sure," said Barbie. "Are you up to it?"

"Sure," Valeria said with a smile.

Finally, the bags appeared on the carousel. They carried them to the car and were soon driving down the highway. Because of the delays, they were now in rush-hour traffic. Bumper-to-bumper, the cars crawled along. And it was nearly six o'clock!

"Will you make it on time?" Valeria asked.

"I'll be a little late," said Barbie. "But I'll be ready by eight."

Suddenly, the car made a strange sound. It sputtered and then—with a long, heart-breaking wheeze—the engine died.

Barbie tried to start it up again. Clink-clunk, the car replied. Behind them, drivers honked.

Barbie got out and lifted the hood. She checked the radiator and the hoses. Everything looked fine to her. Just then, something cold brushed her cheek. Looking up, Barbie saw that the sky was filled with snow flurries. Oh, no, she thought. I hope this doesn't turn into a storm.

The next thing she knew, Mr. Stavinsky was standing beside her. "I mechanic. I will fix," he told her.

"You're a mechanic? Great!" said Barbie. She ran around to her trunk and took out a case of tools. "Here," she said, handing the case to Mr. Stavinsky.

Barbie got back behind the wheel of the car. "Do you have bad snowstorms?" Valeria asked, worried.

"They can get pretty bad," Barbie said, looking up at the gray sky. The snow was falling harder now. “This doesn’t look good,” she admitted. “But we have one lucky break—that your father is a mechanic.”

“Maybe, maybe not,” said Valeria. “He is a tractor and farm equipment mechanic. Maybe a car isn’t too different.”

Barbie crossed her fingers. “Here’s hoping,” she said.

9

A Daring Move

"There is no excuse for this!" Ivan thundered. It was ten minutes to eight, and Barbie had just walked in.

Barbie didn't have time to explain. She kept walking toward her dressing room.

"How could you be so late?" he continued.

Barbie didn't like being screamed at. The last two hours had been difficult enough. Mr. Stavinsky had gotten the car started. But it had died again. By the time the tow truck came, it was after seven. From the service station, they'd taken a cab. But the snow had made traffic crawl. "Let me tell you something, Ivan," Barbie began in self-defense. She was about to tell him she'd been picking up his parents. But then she stopped. She wasn't going to let a moment's anger spoil everything.

"I've had a tough day. I'll explain later," she said instead. "Now, if you'll excuse me, I have to get dressed."

Mrs. Hill was waiting for her in the dressing room. "At last!" the woman cried when Barbie entered.

In the first act, Barbie wore a lovely party dress. Mrs. Hill unzipped the costume. It had a calf-length skirt of pink tulle with a zigzag hemline. "Step into it! Hurry!" Mrs. Hill urged her.

The makeup lady ran in and quickly made up Barbie's face. Then Barbie tied up her white toe shoes.

Barbie hurried to the stage. She waited in the wings. She had about three minutes to do some quick warm-up exercises, and then the curtain rose. On cue, she danced out onto the stage.

Under the bright lights, Barbie could barely see the members of the audience. But she was very aware of them. It was as if they added their own energy to the performance. Barbie danced as never before.

"Wonderful, Barbie," said Ivan at the end of the first act. He had forgotten all about her lateness.

In the second act Barbie danced alone, and then with Ivan. Then it was time for Ivan's solo. He spun through the air to loud applause.

While all eyes were on Ivan, Barbie slipped away. She raced back to her dressing room. As they had planned, Valeria was waiting for her.

With lightning speed, Valeria helped Barbie unzip the nightgown costume. Then she undressed and quickly stepped into it. "It fits perfectly," Barbie observed.

Valeria smiled brightly. "Good luck," Barbie said as Valeria hurried onstage.

Slowly, Barbie pulled on a simple black dress. She'd hung it in her dressing room closet the day before. Barbie then watched from the wings as Valeria joined Ivan at the center of the stage. Barbie studied Ivan's face. At first, he didn't even seem to realize there had been a switch.

Then Valeria twirled into his arms.

Suddenly, a radiant smile spread across his face. It was a smile of complete joy.

The audience didn't seem to know the difference. Barbie and Valeria looked so alike!

Ivan and Valeria amazed the audience. Their last dance together was about parting—Clara must leave The Nutcracker Prince. Barbie saw that both Valeria and Ivan were crying as they danced. They really know how it feels to say good-bye, she thought.

When the ballet was over, the audience leapt to its feet and clapped wildly. "Bravo!" several people cried out. "Bravo!"

One of the dancers playing a jester presented Valeria with a dozen red roses. At once, both Valeria and Ivan looked toward the wings and spotted Barbie.

Holding out his hand, Ivan walked over to Barbie. "You are a remarkable person, Barbie," he said, leading her onstage.

A gasp spread through the crowd as Barbie and Valeria stood side by side.

"Tonight, Clara was played by my sister, Valeria Stavinsky," Ivan said. "And by a bright new talent, Barbie!"

Valeria took her bouquet and handed six roses to Barbie.

The crowd went wild. When the curtain came down, people didn't stop clapping. Together, Ivan, Valeria and Barbie walked out for their curtain calls. Smiling and crying at once, Ivan and Valeria threw kisses to the audience.

After the final curtain call, the house lights were turned up and people began to leave.

Ivan and Valeria stood in the hallway

outside the dressing rooms, hugging and talking happily in Russian.

Barbie was about to get her coat when she saw the director storming toward them. He was red-faced with fury.

"Would someone tell me what that was all about!" he yelled. "I could have you fired for that stunt, Barbie!"

10

Twin Stars

"We owe it all to Barbie," Valeria told the reporters. Before Tony could say another word, they had gathered around Barbie, Ivan and Valeria.

Pictures were taken, video cameras whirred, mikes were held up. "Barbie, what gave you the idea to do this?" a reporter asked.

"Since Valeria and I look so much alike, I thought it would be a wonderful surprise for Ivan," she replied.

"It was the best surprise of my life," Ivan said.

At that moment, Ivan spotted his parents standing off in the corner. He broke away from the reporters and ran to them. The three of them hugged for a long time.

Leaving Valeria to talk to the reporters, Barbie excused herself. She went to meet Ken, who stood holding a huge bunch of flowers. "You were wonderful," he whispered, hugging her.

"Thank you," said Barbie, taking the flowers. "But Tony is so angry. He might even fire me."

"Don't worry," said Tony, coming up behind them. "I was angry because you should have told me what was going on."

"Sorry," said Barbie. "I didn't think of that."

"It's all right," the director said. "Look at those reporters. Thanks to you, we are big news. This will hit the front page. We'll surely have to add more shows."

"So, I'm not fired?" asked Barbie.

"Of course not," said Tony. "Besides, how could I fire a ballerina who dances the way you do? How would you feel about dancing every other show? Valeria would dance the others."

"It sounds perfect," Barbie said.

As Tony walked away, Barbie saw Skipper coming toward her. With her were Barbie's good friends, Midge, Alan, Kira and Christie.

"Come on, superstar, we'll take you out to dinner," Kira suggested.

"No," said Barbie. "There's a big party at the restaurant across the street. You are all my guests."

At the restaurant, a fancy meal had been set out. There was shrimp, crab legs and a special Russian caviar. Everyone had a great time.

"Barbie, can I ask you a favor?" asked Kira.

"Sure," Barbie replied. "What is it?"

"I'd like to take a drive up to see my Uncle Ben in a couple of weeks. He lives up in the mountains, and he's all by himself. With the holidays coming, I think it would be nice if someone visited him."

"That's kind of you," said Barbie. "Do you want me to feed your cats?"

"No. It's a bigger favor than that," said Kira.

"I was hoping that you could come with me. Uncle Ben can be quite cranky. It would be a lot more fun for me if I had a friend along."

Barbie looked over to where the Stavinskys stood together. Ivan had his arm around his sister. The family was laughing and having a wonderful time.

"I don't think Valeria would mind taking my shows," said Barbie to Kira. "I'd love to go."

"I'm warning you," laughed Kira. "Uncle Ben makes Scrooge look like Santa."

"Don't worry," said Barbie. "We'll be able to cheer him up."

Everyone stayed up very late. A little after midnight, Tony held up an early copy of the morning paper. A big picture of Ivan, Valeria and Barbie was on the front page.

"Here's the headline," he read. "'Twin Stars Shine Bright.'" He went on to read the story. The writer called Barbie "remarkably unselfish" and predicted that she would be as great a dancer as Valeria Stavinsky. "Her beauty and energy lit the stage," he wrote.

"So, what do you think, star?" Ken asked Barbie. "Would you like to become the greatest ballerina of your time?"

Barbie slipped her arm through his. "I don't know," she said seriously. "Becoming a truly great dancer takes a lot of work. It has to be your whole life. There are still so many other things I'd like to try."

"That's going to be a problem," said Ken. "Because you're good at everything you try. How will you ever know what you're best at?"

Barbie squeezed his arm lovingly. "I know one thing. No matter what else happens to me, I'll never forget this night."

Ken and Barbie looked over at the Stavinskys. Ivan caught sight of them. He smiled and blew Barbie a kiss.

"You can be sure the Stavinskys will never forget you," said Ken.

"Valeria and Ivan are amazing dancers, aren't they?" said Barbie.

Ken hugged her. "There's no one more amazing than you, Barbie," he said.